This book belongs to:

....

PUBLISHED BY PETER HADDOCK LIMITED,
BRIDLINGTON, ENGLAND
PRINTED IN ITALY
ISBN O 7105 0378 4

ALICE IN WONDERLAND

Alice was very tired of sitting doing nothing. She was thinking about making a daisy chain but the hot day was making her sleepy, when suddenly a white rabbit ran past. The rabbit took out a watch from his waistcoat pocket and muttered "I'm late, I'm late," and rushed on.

"How very strange," thought Alice and got up to follow the rabbit, just in time to see it pop down a rabbit hole.

Alice followed the rabbit down the hole and found herself falling in the darkness.
Down and down she fell. She began to feel sleepy, the tunnel seemed never-ending. Suddenly she landed with a thud, but fortunately was not hurt. In front of her was a long passage and she just caught sight of the white rabbit still running. Alice followed and found herself in a hall.
On every wall were many doors. All of them were locked. On a little table was a tiny key. It fitted a door just a few centimetres high.

But how could a tall girl like Alice get through a door a few centimetres high? On the table with the tiny key was a bottle with a label on it. It said "Drink Me."

But Alice wasn't going to do that in a hurry — one never knows what might be in a bottle left lying about. However, it wasn't marked "Poison" so Alice decided to taste a little. "Oh," she said to herself, "I'm getting smaller and smaller."

This cheered Alice up as she realised that now she could get throught the tiny door.

Now that Alice was the right size, she ran to the door and tried to open it, but, poor Alice had put the key back on the table and now she was much too small to reach it. Alice could see the key through the glass table top and tried to climb up the leg but it was too slippery. She gave up and sat down and cried.
Then Alice decided that crying would get her no-where and as she looked up, she saw a little box under the table. Inside the box were some cakes and the currants on the top spelt the words "Eat Me." So Alice ate them and waited to see whether she would get bigger or smaller.

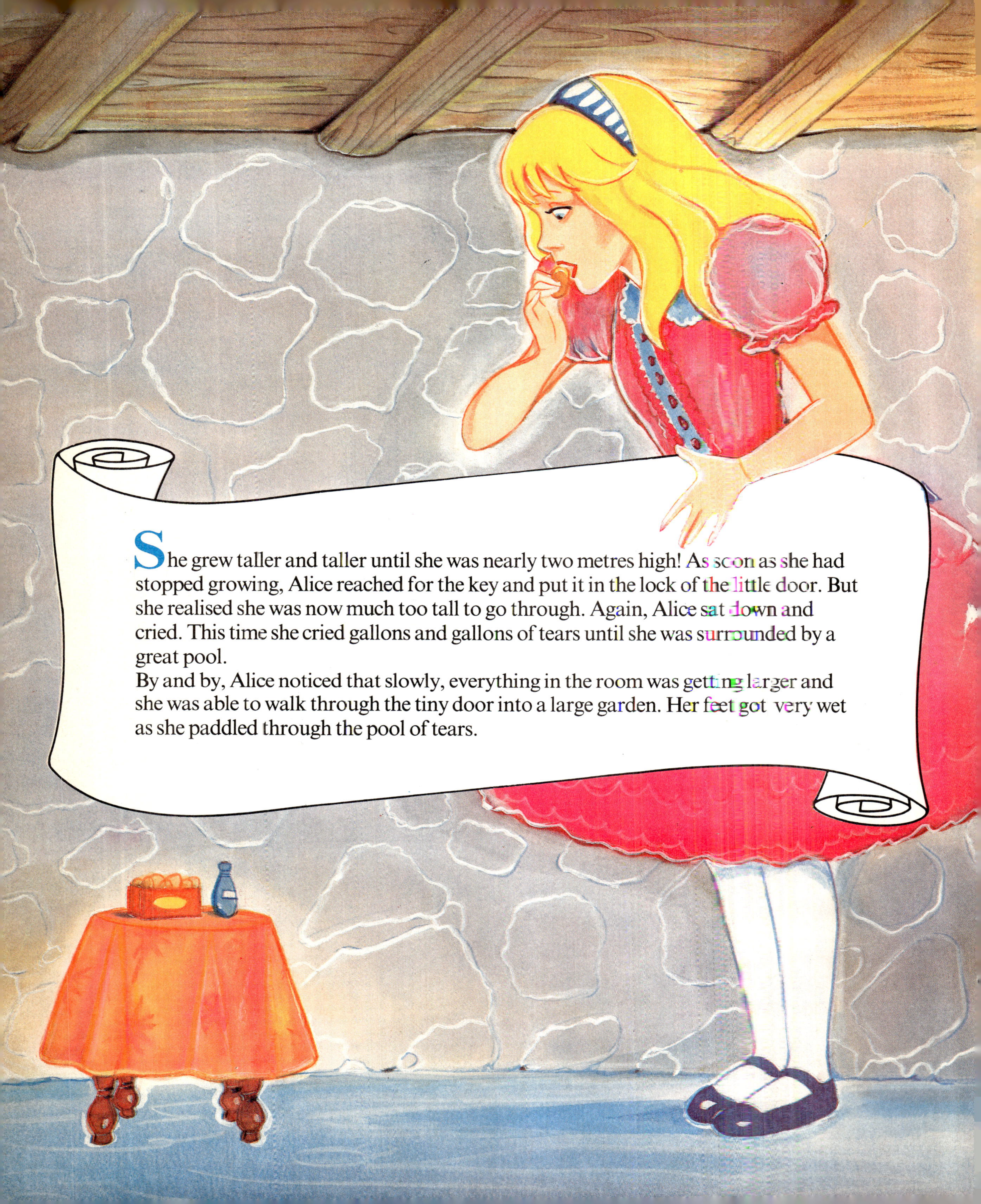

She grew taller and taller until she was nearly two metres high! As soon as she had stopped growing, Alice reached for the key and put it in the lock of the little door. But she realised she was now much too tall to go through. Again, Alice sat down and cried. This time she cried gallons and gallons of tears until she was surrounded by a great pool.

By and by, Alice noticed that slowly, everything in the room was getting larger and she was able to walk through the tiny door into a large garden. Her feet got very wet as she paddled through the pool of tears.

There were quite a few animals swimming about in the pool, an eaglet and a dodo were nearby and Alice had quite a long conversation with the mouse who was paddling at the edge.
Through the garden she walked and soon came across a large caterpillar who was sitting on a mushroom, smoking a hookah pipe.

Alice spoke to the caterpillar and she tried to explain to him that she kept either growing or shrinking. She said that she would like to be the size she started with, but couldn't remember what that was.

"One side will make you taller, the other will make you smaller," said the caterpillar and disappeared into the garden.

"One side of what?" asked Alice, but it was too late, the caterpillar had gone.

"I suppose he must mean the mushroom. I'll try it, anyway," said Alice.

Alice walked on through the garden, nibbling at the mushroom. Eventually, she made herself her original height.
Soon she came across a tiny house just about fifteen centimetres high. Alice ate some mushroom to shrink a little. Suddenly, a footman came running out of the wood with a large envelope in his hand. He gave this to the butler who opened the door of the little house and told him that it was an invitation for the Duchess to play croquet. When the footman had gone, Alice went up to the house and knocked on the door. As the butler opened it, a large plate flew past them and in the confusion Alice slipped into the house. She found herself in the kitchen.

The Duchess was sitting on a stool and a large cat with a huge smile on its face was by the fireside.
"Please tell me," said Alice to the Duchess, "why your cat is grinning like that."
"It's a Cheshire cat," replied the Duchess, "and that's why!"
Then the Duchess said that she was now going to play croquet with the Queen, so Alice went out into the garden and set off to walk a little further.
The Cheshire cat was in a tree watching her and grinning.

After a while Alice found a rose garden. There were three gardeners painting the white roses red.

"Why are you doing that?" asked Alice.

"The Queen wanted red roses and we planted white ones. If she finds out she'll chop off our heads," replied one of the gardeners who looked remarkably like a playing card.

Alice retraced her steps and spoke gently to the cat which grinned even more. The cat had very long claws and lots of teeth so Alice decided it ought to be treated with respect.

"What sort of people live that way?" pointed Alice.

"The Mad Hatter lives there and the March Hare lives that way," replied the cat. "But it doesn't matter which way you go, we're all mad here." With that the cat disappeared.

Alice walked on further and came across the March Hare's house. Outside, a table was set for a tea party and there sat the Mad Hatter, the March Hare and the Dormouse.

As Alice sat down at the table, the Dormouse woke up and began to tell a complicated story which Alice couldn't understand, so she left the tea party in disgust.

One of the gardeners suddenly called out "The Queen! The Queen!" and they all threw themselves flat on their faces.
Alice recognised the White Rabbit in the Queen's entourage, but he didn't notice her.
The procession stopped opposite Alice and the Queen of Hearts asked who Alice was.
Alice was very polite but thought to herself that it was silly being polite to a pack of cards.
"Can you play croquet?" demanded the Queen to Alice. Alice replied that she could.
So Alice joined the procession.

The Queen shouted to everyone to get to their places and the game began. It was a curious game of croquet; the mallets were flamingos and the croquet balls were live hedgehogs. Alice had great difficulty with her flamingo. Just as she had it lined up with the hedgehog, the flamingo turned round to look at her with a puzzled expression which made her laugh. Sometimes the hedgehog uncurled itself and walked off in the opposite direction.

Alice soon came to the conclusion that it was a very difficult game indeed. Everyone played at once, arguing all the time and fought for the hedgehogs which were in short supply.

The Queen kept getting very angry and was constantly shouting "Off with his head!"
Nearby was a Gryphon asleep in the sun. The Queen woke him up and gave him instructions to take Alice to see the Mock Turtle. When they found the turtle, he was sitting on a rock looking very sad. He began to tell them all about his lessons under the sea and his teachers. The Mock Turtle then sang his "Beautiful Soup" song but this was interrupted by a cry in the distance.
"The Trial's beginning!"
"Come on," cried the Gryphon and hurried off with Alice.

The King and Queen of Hearts were there, surrounded by birds and animals. The Knave was in chains, guarded by two soldiers. The White Rabbit stood nearby and in the middle of the court was the evidence - a plate of jam tarts.

Alice saw that the King was wearing a wig so he must be the judge. She was just about to ask the Gryphon what was happening when the White Rabbit called for silence.

The White Rabbit accused the Knave of stealing the tarts and called the Mad Hatter as a witness. He was not much use and so he was dismissed. It was then that Alice realised that she was beginning to get taller.

The White Rabbit called the next witness.

"Alice."

Alice quite forgot that she was her normal size and, as she stood up, she knocked the jury box over, upsetting the jury into the crowd. It took some time to get them back into their places and to find all their slates and pencils.
The King asked Alice what she knew about the knave stealing the tarts. Alice replied that she knew nothing at all about it. This upset the King and he ordered that all people over a mile high had to leave the courtroom. He said that this was in the rules - number forty-two to be exact. Alice said that he was making it up. The White Rabbit interrupted with some fresh evidence.